THE
CRYSTAL
APPLE

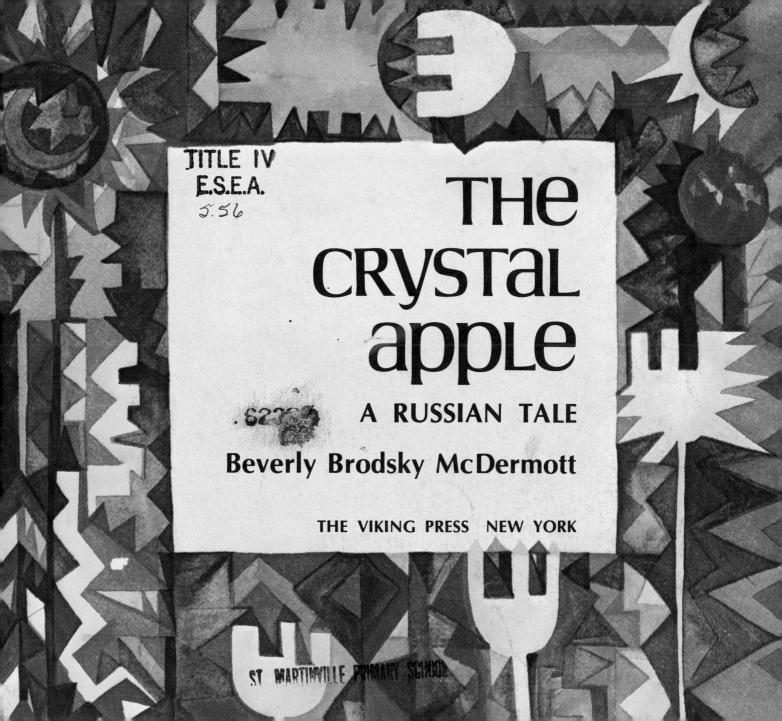

THE CRYSTAL apple

A RUSSIAN TALE

Beverly Brodsky McDermott

THE VIKING PRESS   NEW YORK

FIRST EDITION

Copyright © 1974 by Beverly Brodsky McDermott
All rights reserved
First published in 1974 by The Viking Press, Inc.
625 Madison Avenue, New York, N.Y. 10022
Published simultaneously in Canada by
The Macmillan Company of Canada Limited
Printed in U.S.A.

1 2 3 4 5 78 77 76 75 74

Library of Congress Cataloging in Publication Data
McDermott, Beverly Brodsky. The crystal apple.
Summary: Three sisters receive gifts from their father,
but Marusha's crystal apple proves to be a greater gift
than she had imagined.
I. Title. PZ7.M143Cr [E] 74–3312

ISBN 0–670–25052–x

For Gerald, with love

Sasha, Masha, and Marusha were sisters.
They worked in the fields each day.
They collected the sunflower seeds
and gathered the wheat.

In the evening
while her sisters slept
Marusha liked to dream
and imagine.

One day Father prepared
to leave for market.
He called his daughters.
"What gift can I bring for each?"
   They thought for a while.
Sasha asked for silken threads,
Masha a string of the finest pearls,
and Marusha asked for a crystal apple.
   "A crystal apple? I will try,"
Father said,
"but crystal apples are rare."

So, off he rode

until he came to market.

Many days passed,
and the sisters continued
to work in the fields.

At last father returned
bearing the gifts,
even the crystal apple.
Marusha and her sisters
thanked their father.

Marusha placed the apple
on the table and looked deep inside.
She saw a rainbow—
the cathedrals of Moscow—
the forests in winter—

the ships on the River Volga—
even a sturgeon,
asleep in a deep pool.

Sasha and Masha became curious.
One night they took the apple
and looked inside.
But they saw nothing.
They shook it and spun it
until—

Oh!

The next day, Marusha cried.
Father said, "Don't be unhappy.
Imagination is a precious gift."
They went to the river.
Marusha gazed into the water.

She looked up at the clouds

and into
the deep
forest.

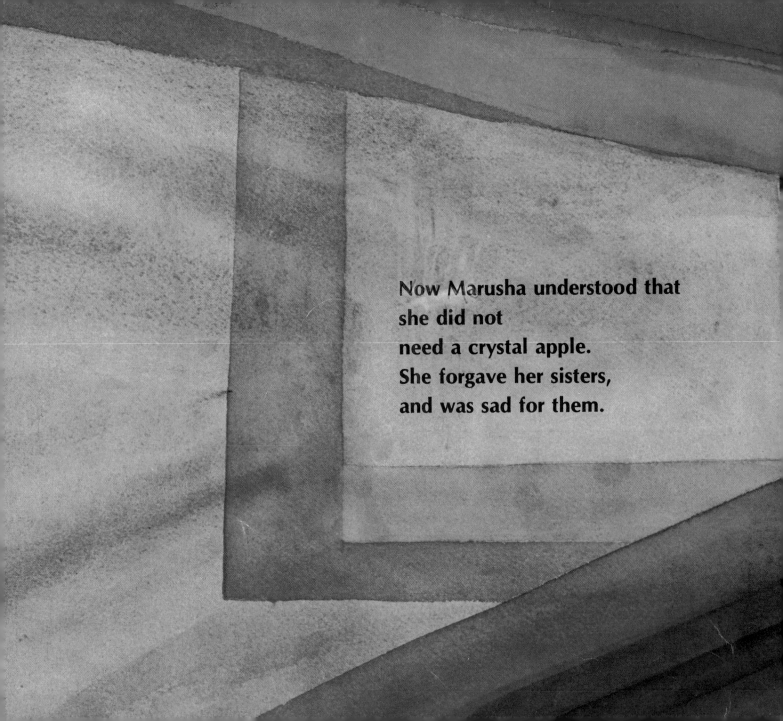

Now Marusha understood that
she did not
need a crystal apple.
She forgave her sisters,
and was sad for them.

About the Artist

BEVERLY BRODSKY McDERMOTT is a graduate of
Brooklyn College, where she studied art under
Ad Reinhardt. She has traveled widely in Europe and
now makes her home in the Hudson River Valley with
her husband, Gerald McDermott. About her work,
Ms. McDermott says:

"My interest in art developed during childhood. For
me it was a means of transforming my world of
tenements and pushcarts into the unobtainable world
of the theater. Over and over again I painted the
dancers, the scenery, and the costumes, making these
things part of my world. This desire to paint, combined
with an awareness of my Russian heritage, led to the
creation of THE CRYSTAL APPLE, a story about a young
girl who sees the world through the power of her
imagination."

About the Book

The paintings for THE CRYSTAL APPLE were done in
gouache, water color, and with Luma Dyes. The art
was reproduced in four-color process, and the text
type is Optima Semibold.

DATE DUE			
W			